OSCAR
THE ORGO

For Olivia, Ian and Lewis - RJF

For Eleanor and Iris - FF

ORGO PRESS
First published in 2020 by Orgo Press

Text copyright © R.J. Furness 2020
Illustrations copyright © Fiona Fletcher 2020

Written By
R.J. Furness

Illustrated By
Fiona Fletcher

THAT'S WHAT FRIENDS ARE FOR!

Have you ever met Oscar the orgo?
He's a creature you might not know.
With a long, thin neck, and only two legs,
he tends to hang out in the snow.

Hold on—that's not really true.
He hasn't yet left his cave.
Oscar was only born yesterday,
And he isn't quite feeling that brave.

Yesterday, when Oscar was born,
he'd been busy singing his song.
There wasn't time to play in the snow.
He had gliders to move along.

When the sun came up this morning.
Oscar awoke with a start.
His cave was very noisy,
like the world was falling apart.

'What's going on?' asked Oscar,
blinking his sleepy eyes.
'Breakfast first!' Mum answered.
'You're in for a big surprise.'

'I like surprises,' said Oscar,
munching his food in his nest.
'Being an orgo is awesome.
It certainly is the best!'

When Oscar finished his
orchids,
Mum gave him a big friendly
smile.
'Today,' she said, 'you'll learn
something new.
Today is your running trial.'

Oscar was feeling puzzled.
'Running? Please, tell me more.'
'It's what we do,' replied his mum.
'It's an orgo thing for sure.'

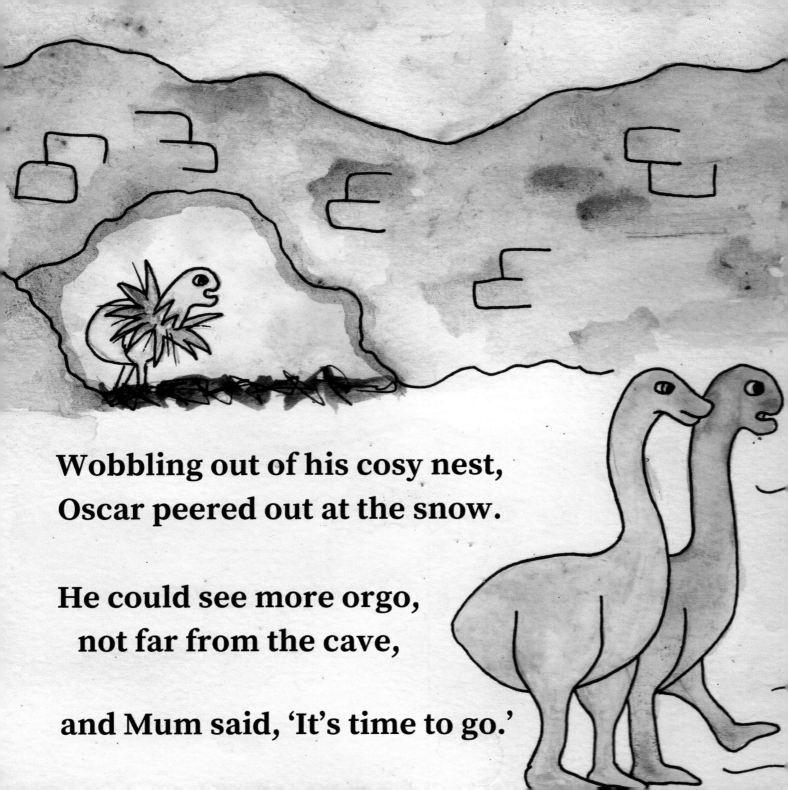

Wobbling out of his cosy nest,
Oscar peered out at the snow.

He could see more orgo,
 not far from the cave,

and Mum said, 'It's time to go.'

**Oscar's toes turned icy cold
when he stepped outside his home.
'Blimey,' he cried, following Mum.
'It's freezing. I don't mean to moan.'**

'You'll soon warm up, I promise you dear.'
Mum grinned as she turned her head.
'Okay, Mum. I'm sure that's true.
But I think I prefer my bed.'

When they reached the other orgo,
Mum introduced Oscar with pride.
'It's nice to meet you,' everyone said.
But Oscar was trying to hide.

'There's nothing to fear,' one orgo said.
'All you need to do is run.'
'But, why?' Oscar queried, squashed
behind Mum.
'I'm not sure it sounds like fun.'

The orgo laughed at Oscar,
who was starting to
feel quite scared.

'It's very easy,' another
one called,
'as long as you're well
prepared.'

'Here,' said Mum. 'Let me show you how.

Put one foot in front of the other.'

'Okay then, Mum,' Oscar agreed.

'I'll trust you because you're my mother.'

Oscar could see other orgo pups,
copying their parents in style.

Dashing around in circles,
excited for their running trial.

'My name's Snowflake,' a small orgo said.
Her fleece was shiny and white.
When she appeared next to Oscar,
she gave him quite a fright!

Before Oscar had a chance to speak,
Snowflake dashed off in a rush.
'That's how you do it!' exclaimed his mum.
'But watch out for the slippery slush.'

'Right,' said Oscar, determined at last,
'I can do this. I'm sure you're not wrong.'
Following the other young orgo,
Oscar hurried along.

'You start over here,' a grown-up said.
'Then you run all the way to that rock.'
'I'll race you,' giggled Snowflake,
as she stood at the starting block.

'Fine by me,' Oscar declared,
going along with the flow.
'Great,' said the adult orgo.
'On your marks. Get set. Go!'

Sprinting away from the starting line,
Snowflake took an early lead.
Oscar, meanwhile, stumbled around,
trying to pick up speed.

'Come on, Oscar. You're almost there.'
Mum shouted from nearby.

'I'm not sure I'm ready,'
wailed Oscar.
'I'm not gonna tell a lie.'

It didn't take long for Snowflake to vanish,
hidden amongst the snow.
There was no way for Oscar to win their race.
His running was far too slow.

Seconds later, snorts rose from the crowd as they cheered for Snowflake's success.

She had already beaten Oscar,
even though he had tried his best.

Mum trotted over as quick as she could,
while Oscar took a break.
'Well done, son. I'm proud of you.
I hope your feet don't ache.'

'I'm not quite finished,' Oscar replied,
trudging through the snow.
'I might not have won, but that isn't important.
Sorry. I need to go.'

Mum moved away while Oscar
walked on,
until he completed the race.
Full of joy, she trailed behind,
with a smile upon her face.

Meeting Snowflake at the rock,
Oscar said, 'That was fantastic.'
'Really?' asked Snowflake, appearing surprised.
'Are you sure you're not being sarcastic?'

'No,' said Oscar, shaking his head.
'But my speed was a total disaster.'
Snowflake replied, 'It's just practice you need—
I can show you how to go faster.'

'That would be brilliant!'
Oscar said.
'And I think we should
race again.
But if you'll excuse me, I
must go home.
I have singing to do
before then.'

With a look of confusion,
Snowflake turned.

'Singing?
I'd love to hear more.'

'I'll show you,' said Oscar.
'Now that we're friends.
Because that's what
friends are for.'

About The Author

R. J. Furness has been passionate about great stories since he was able to read. At an early age, he would frequently create new characters, worlds and creatures, then write crazy tales all about them. However, until now, he has always kept those ideas completely secret. After having a lifelong interest in animals, music and anything spawned from pure imagination, R.J.'s first love is now his wife and children. Over time, he has also developed an overwhelming desire for mugs of tea and good biscuits to dunk. He lives in Southport, England, with his family, a dog and several fish, chickens and quails.

Find out more about R.J. Furness and his extraordinary worlds...

www.rjfurness.com

or please come and say hello on social media...

Twitter: @rjfurness
Facebook: furnesswrites

About The Illustrator

Fiona has been a keen artist since the days of drawing on her parent's walls as a toddler. Through school, she always pursued the artistic and creative classes which allowed her to find her own flare. In 2017, after having two children, Fiona began her artistic business, Menagerie Of Mayhem, painting in bright rainbow colours and finding her place in the art world. All this, whilst also being able to spend all the time in the world with her daughters, going on school trips, days out at the zoo and more!

Explore more of Fiona's work on Etsy, and get your exclusive Oscar merchandise...
menagerieofmayhem.etsy.com

Find Fiona on Facebook - www.facebook.com/menagerieofmayhem
Follow Fiona on Instagram - www.instagram.com/menagerie_of_mayhem

For More Orgo Adventures, Try The Orgo Runners Series!

Suitable For Readers Aged 6 And Over

Watch Out For...

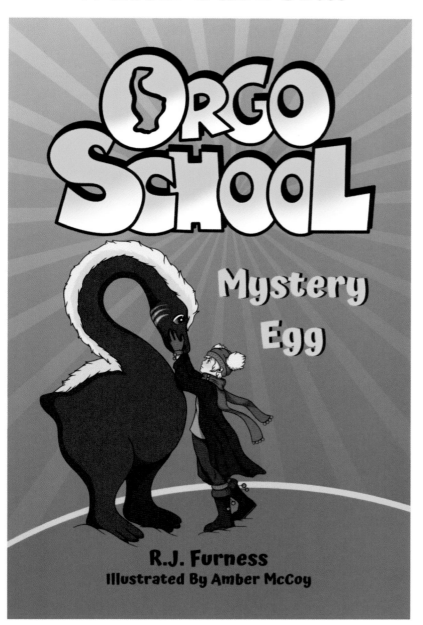

ORGO SCHOOL

Mystery Egg

R.J. Furness

Illustrated By Amber McCoy

A Brand New Adventure!

Perfect For Children Aged 4+

Printed in Great Britain
by Amazon